Cop

CW00393702

Tom Martin

Published by G. Heathcote

All Rights Reserved

Artwork

Courtesy of

Pixabay

First Edition: March 2016

Printed in the United Kingdom

Thank you

Margaret Wilson

John Crookes

Daveen Heathcote

2

Contents

HOW TO BAKE A MAN

Introduction

In times past it was believed that food held properties which could invoke feelings of love, passion, health and protection. All around the world each culture has its own secret recipes and rituals. When used in combination, certain ingredients were said to have an almost magical effect. The wedding cake, the birthday cake and the christening cake are all symbols of a tradition that has been followed for centuries. We light candles and wishes are made before the cake is eaten, without realising we are performing an age old rite. One where we wish happiness for the newly weds, a healthy life and many more years for the person who celebrates their birthday and offer love and protection for the children at their christening or naming days.

In the following pages we take the beliefs of our ancestors and mix tradition with an element of the new.

We all have our own ideas of what we would like our perfect partner to be. As individuals we want different things from the person we intend spending our lives with. Some search for a soul mate, full of kindness and love for their fellow man, while others want a successful, business tycoon as their other half. The qualities we look for in a partner are unique to every one of us. With this in mind, we created a list of ingredients which cover many of the virtues we seek in a partner and put them together to produce easy to follow recipes. Each cake can be tailored to your own needs. While you can bake your wishing cake on your own, we found it far more entertaining and fun to get together with friends and have a baking party. There is a recipe for everyone, including those who have already found their special person. After all, we can never have enough love or passion. Whatever your heart is searching for, we have a recipe just for you.

 While it is impossible to guarantee the wishes you make will come true. We are certain you will enjoy the adventure. You can experiment with our ideas and put into practice a little magic and see what happens. One thing we can predict, it's great fun!

Three elements which help to make the recipes work.

- The first and most important is that you believe.
- Secondly, is the gathering together of friends. The ones who will throw themselves into the spirit of adventure and share in the magic of creating something unique.
- The third and most vital element is that you love cake!

Preparing for your Party

Prepare your table before the guests arrive. An attractive paper tablecloth will protect your table and can be disposed of at the end of the mixing. Place new white candles in safety holders on the table When the mixing begins keep the lights low and work by candle light where possible. This will give atmosphere to the magic you are making. While the mixing is taking place, background music should be low and appropriate to the mood you are creating. Your party will be dedicated to finding lovers, potential partners or enhancing already stable relationships for yourself and your guests, music can help deliver strong emotions which need to be focused during the mixing of the cake.

 As the host of the party, provide a large mixing bowl to mix the main cake ingredients in. This will be equally shared out amongst your guest, ready for them to include their own personal ingredients. Paper plates to cut and assemble their cake decorations can be used to prevent a build up of washing up afterwards.

Before the cake cases are filled, make sure each guest writes their name on the bottom of their case. Or use different coloured cases, (especially important if any of your guests have an intolerance or allergy to nuts) to avoid any confusion as to whose cake is whose.

The cakes are tailored for each guest and their requirements, it would add another dimension all together if the cakes got mixed up and the wrong ones were eaten. Who knows where that could lead!

Once the cake mixing is completed and the cakes are placed in the oven, change the music and *party.*

Just before the cakes are taken from the oven, change the music again to allow your guests to focus their concentration on their projects. Allow time for the cakes to cool. The decoration of the cake is an important part of the proceedings. Once the decoration has been completed and the table has been cleared the final part of the ceremony takes place. The eating of the cake. This plays a vital role in the success of the ritual.

Each cake should be placed on a clean paper plate and the guests should be sitting comfortably and relaxed in order to devote all their thoughts to what they want their cake to achieve. Ask your guest to imagine what they want their cake to help bring as they eat. They should savour each mouthful and think hard on what they have asked for. When the cake eating has been completed. The ritual is over and the party then becomes a celebration of the things to come.

Keeping the guest list to twelve and under offers a more intimate experience for you and your invited guests. Although it is your party and you can do what you want to.

Why not add an extra fun element to the night by providing a prize for the person who brings the most original apron. The craziest, rudest, cutest apron, etc., wins. Remember to mention this to your guest when inviting them to your party. Of course, no party would be complete without one or two bottles of wine. You can provide the refreshments or ask your guests to bring along their favourite tipple. Don't forget to provide soft drinks or tea and coffee for those guests who don't drink or who might be driving.

Host Requirement

- Wooden Spoon
- Large mixing bowl
- Apron
- Paper Plates
- Paper Napkins
- Main ingredients for the cake mix
- Six or twelve cup baking tray (Depending on how many guests you have invited)
- Paper cake cases
- Piping Bag or Spatula
- A suitable size table
- White Candles with safety holders

What your guests will need

Ask your invited guests to bring along a mixing bowl, a wooden spoon and an apron. In order to ensure each guest has the right ingredients, they will need to chose a recipe before your party. This gives your guest a chance to study what they want in their prospective partner and bring along the ingredients they wish to use. Remember to tell them about the apron competition.

- Mixing bowl
- Wooden Spoon
- Apron
- Ingredients and decorations for their cake
- Small birthday cake candle in the appropriate colour (The candle must not have been used before)

Recipes which include nuts or biscuits.

Pestle and Mortar
Clean plastic bag
Rolling Pin

The power of togetherness helps make the magic stronger.

In the main recipe, the ingredients used, all have a special meaning.

- Self Raising Flour - Love
- Caster Sugar - Sweetness
- Eggs - Faithfulness
- Milk - Strength
- Unsalted Butter - Kindness

Main Recipe

The host of the party can mix the ingredients for the main recipe. These ingredients provide the base for your individual cakes.

Makes 12 cakes

Ingredients

150g self raising flour

3 eggs (Beaten)

150g sugar

150g butter

1 tablespoon Milk

1 teaspoon vanilla extract

Vanilla Butter Cream Icing

175g butter

300g icing sugar

1 tablespoon Milk

1 teaspoon vanilla extract

Add your chosen food colouring.

Method

Preheat oven 180C/200C fan / gas mark 4

Cream the butter and sugar until soft and fluffy

Add beaten Eggs gradually

Add flour gradually

Add vanilla extract and milk.

When the mixture has been mixed, the host will stir the contents clockwise. The bowl is then passed to each guest who in turn will stir the mixture once clockwise. This is the beginning of the magic. When the stirring has been completed, divide the mixture equally among your guests.

Guest will now follow their individual recipes. Adding to the mix any ingredients required before the baking.

To avoid any confusion later, ask your guest to write their names on the bottom of their paper baking cases before filling. Or use different coloured cake cases.

When the individual cake has been prepared

Place in oven for 15/20 minutes.

While the cakes are baking, mix the icing.

Remove cakes from oven when golden brown/springy to touch

Place cakes on wire rack to cool.

Icing

Beat butter until soft and smooth. Use either a fork or spatula. Gradually mix in the icing sugar, stir regularly

Add vanilla extract and milk. Mix until light and creamy.

The host then stirs the icing mixture once, clockwise. Pass the bowl around until each guest has stirred the mixture once, clockwise.

When the cakes have been allowed to cool completely.

Each guest can spoon or pipe icing onto their individual cake.

Decorating Your Wishing Cake

Decorating your individual cake with the fruits, nuts or chocolate you have chosen is a most vital part of the ritual. The ingredients you pick all represent a virtue. The ingredients you chose to decorate your cake are important. Each piece has a meaning and will help predict the outcome of your wish.

Numbers also hold power and have special meanings. The amounts you place on your cake will have an effect on the outcome.

When the decoration of the cake has been completed, leave to set for 30 minutes.

Ceremony of Wishes

An important part of the ritual is the ceremony of wishes. The candles are placed on the cake and lit. Each guest will concentrate on what their cake represents. The power of belief is essential at this point. The individual should take a few minutes to

imagine all they are wishing for to come true. With this in mind – blow out the candle.

Watch as your wish swirls in the wisps of smoke before disappearing out into the atmosphere.

The last and most vital part of the ceremony is the eating of the cake. Savour each mouthful, concentrating on what you are hoping for. Once the cake has been eaten the ritual is complete.

Your search for your heart's desire has now begun.

Believe and all things are possible.

The power of thought is a potent tool.

Wishes really can come true.

How to Attract a Soul Mate

Try this recipe if you are looking for a life partner. That special someone to make you feel complete.

Ingredients

Raisins

Strawberry

Milk Chocolate or Milk chocolate chips
Cherry

Before baking

Add 6 raisins to your mixture. (Stir clockwise)

Place cake in oven for 15/20 minutes.

Once baked, allow cake to cool. Add icing.

To Decorate

1 strawberry, do not cut, to be kept whole

3 small pieces of chocolate or 3 chocolate chips

1 cherry, cut in half

Arrange your ingredients on the cake. Leave to set for 30 minutes.

Place a small orange candle on the cake and light it.

Think of drawing your soul mate to you. Spend a few minutes to concentrate on your goal. Make a wish to find your soul mate. Ask for true love, happiness and harmony.

Blow out candle and remove Whilst

thinking of attracting your soul mate to you, eat cake.

Romance

Try this recipe if you are hoping to add a little more passion into an already ongoing relationship. Or attract a little romance into your life, without the attachment.

Ingredients

Cayenne pepper
Dark chocolate or Dark chocolate chips
Apple
Banana
Red Grape

Before baking

Add one tiny pinch of cayenne pepper
Grate a small amount of orange zest into the mixture (Stir clockwise)
Place cake in oven for 15/20 minutes.

Once baked, allow cake to cool. Add icing.

To Decorate

6 small pieces of dark chocolate or 6 dark
chocolate chips
Take a thin slice of apple and cut into four
1 thin slice of banana, slice in half
1 red grape, cut in half

Arrange your ingredients on the cake. Leave
to set for 30 minutes.

Place a small Pink Candle on cake and light it.

Imagine what you would like your romantic
encounter to be like.

Blow out candle and remove

Sit back and think of your intended lover
while eating your cake.

A Prosperous Lover

Money can't buy you love, but for some, wealth is an aphrodisiac. Try this recipe if you are looking for a little more than love and romance from your partner.

Ingredients
Almond Nut
Pomegranate
Pineapple
Orange
Allspice

Before baking

Place - 1 almond in a clean plastic bag and crush with rolling pin. Use a pestle and mortar to grind almond until it becomes a powder.
Blend into cake mix (Stir clockwise)
Add a tiny sprinkle of allspice to cake mixture
Place cake in oven for 15/20 minutes.

Once baked, allow cake to cool. Add icing.

To Decorate

8 Pomegranate Berries

1 pineapple ring cut into 4 pieces

2 orange segments cut into 6 pieces

Arrange your ingredients on the cake. Leave to set for 30 minutes.

Place a small green candle on the cake and light it.

Think of the lover you would like to attract.

Blow out candle and remove

Sit back and think of your intended lover while   eating your cake.

Virility

Bake this cake for your male partner. Fruit and nuts help stimulate, giving strength and energy. The potency of this recipe can help invoke a stronger sex drive.

Ingredients

Brazil Nut
Walnut
Almond
Strawberry
Banana
Ginger Biscuit

Before Baking

Place - 1 Brazil nut, 1 walnut and 1 almond together in a clean plastic bag and crush with rolling pin. Use a pestle and mortar to grind the nuts into a powder.

Blend powder into your cake mixture. (Stir clockwise)
Place cake in oven for 15/20 minutes.

Once baked, allow cake to cool. Add icing.

To Decorate
2 thin slices of Banana
1 Strawberry cut in half
1 Ginger Biscuit

Arrange your ingredients on the cake. Place ginger biscuit in a clean plastic bag and crush with a rolling pin. Sprinkle crushed biscuit over cake. Leave to set for 30 minutes.

Place a small red candle on the cake and light it
Think of the person your cake is intended for.

Blow out candle and remove
Place cake in a decorative box and give to your partner.

Fun & Flirty

Try this recipe for playful amorous pleasure. Bake this cake to draw an admirer you have a strong sexual attraction to.

Ingredients
Apricot
Cherry
Blackberries
Strawberries
Dark Chocolate

Before baking
Stir your mixture clockwise
Place cake in oven for 15/20 minutes.

Once baked, allow cake to cool. Add icing.

To Decorate
3 thin slices of apricot
1 blackberry cut in half
1 cherry cut in half
1 whole strawberry, do not cut.

5 small pieces of dark chocolate or 5 dark chocolate chips

Arrange your ingredients on the cake. Leave to set for 30 minutes.

Place a small red candle on the cake and light it
Imagine the person you would like to attract.

Blow out candle and remove
Think of having fun and flirting with a lover.

Aphrodisiac for a male

Bake this cake for your male partner, to excite and stimulate. Fruits and spices help to intensify sexual desire.

Ingredients

Cinnamon
Cherry
Blackberry
Banana
Dark Chocolate
Ginger Biscuit

Before baking

Take a small pinch of cinnamon and sprinkle into your cake mixture
Stir your mixture clockwise.

Place cake in oven for 15/20 minutes. Once baked, allow cake to cool. Add icing.

To Decorate

1 cherry cut in half
5 thinly sliced pieces of banana
5 small pieces of dark chocolate or 5 dark chocolate chips
1 whole blackberry, do not cut.

Arrange your ingredients on the cake. Place ginger biscuit in a clean plastic bag and crush with a rolling pin. Sprinkle crushed biscuit over cake. Leave to set for 30 minutes.

Place a small red candle on the cake and light it

Think of the person you have baked the cake for.

Blow out candle and remove

Place cake in a decorative box and give to your partner.

Lust

Try this recipe if you feel your love life needs a boost. You can bake the cake for yourself or for your partner. Better still, make two identical cakes, one for each of you.

Ingredients

Dark chocolate or dark chocolate chips
Strawberries
Raspberries
Red Grape
Blackberries
Apple
Ginger Biscuit

Before baking

Stir your mixture clockwise. Place cake in oven for 15/20 minutes.
Once baked, allow cake to cool. Add icing.

To Decorate

5 small pieces of Dark chocolate or dark chocolate chips.
1Strawberries cut into 3 pieces

1 Raspberry cut in half
1 Blackberry cut in half
1 Red Grape cut in half
1 thinly sliced piece of apple cut in half.

Arrange your ingredients on the cake. Place ginger biscuit in a clean plastic bag and crush with a rolling pin. Sprinkle crushed biscuit over cake. Leave to set for 30 minutes.

Place a small red candle on the cake and light it

Think of the person you have a passionate yearning for. Imagine you and your intended partner having an overwhelming desire for each other.

Blow out the candle and make your wish. Remove Candle.

Thinking of your lover, savour each mouthful of your cake as you eat. Place an identical cake in a decorative box and give to your partner or lover.

Proposal

You both know you love each other and you intend to tie the knot one day. Try this recipe to help nudge things in the right direction.

Ingredients

Orange
Orange zest
Cherries
Apples

Before baking

Stir your mixture clockwise. Place in paper bun case.
Place cake in oven for 15/20 minutes.
Once baked, allow cake to cool. Add icing.

To Decorate

1 Whole Cherry
2 thin slices of apple
1 segment of orange cut in half

Arrange your ingredients on the cake. Grate a small amount of orange zest and sprinkle finely over cake. Leave to set for 30 minutes.

Place a small pink candle on the cake and light it

Imagine your intended proposing.

Blow out the candle and make your wish. Remove Candle.

Think of you and your partner getting married while you eat your cake.
Place an identical cake in a decorative box and give to your partner.

Fertility

Diet is important when trying for a child. Nuts, fruits and seeds are part of a healthy lifestyle. Try this recipe to boost your power of reproduction.

Ingredients
Hazelnut
Almond
Walnut
Red Grape
Sunflower Seed
Apple
Peach

Before baking

Place - 1 hazelnut, 1 almond, 1 walnut, 1 sunflower seed together in a clean plastic bag and crush with rolling pin. Use a pestle and mortar to grind the nuts into a powder.
Blend the crushed mixture into your cake mix. Stir the mixture clockwise.

Place in paper bun case. Place cake in oven for 15/20 minutes.
Once baked, allow cake to cool. Add icing.

To Decorate

1 Red Grape cut in half
2 thin slices of apple cut into 7 pieces
4 thin slices of peach cut into 9 pieces

Arrange your ingredients on the cake. Leave to set for 30 minutes.

Place a small green candle on the cake and light it

Think of you and your partner becoming parents.

Blow out the candle and make your wish. Remove Candle.

Eat your cake and think of being pregnant. Place an identical cake in a decorative box and give to your partner.

Baking for a Friend

Our friends are special and we only want what's best for them. Try this recipe if you have a friend who longs to find that certain someone.

Ingredients

Raisins
Strawberries
Orange
Red grapes
Cherries
Banana
Apple
Dark chocolate

Before baking

Mix 6 Raisins into your cake before baking. Stir clockwise.

Place in paper bun case. Place cake in oven for 15/20 minutes.
Once baked, allow cake to cool. Add icing.

To Decorate

1 Strawberry cut in half
1 segment of Orange cut in half
1 Red grape cut in half
1 Cherry whole
3 thin slices of Banana
1 thin slice of Apple cut into four
6 small pieces of dark chocolate or dark chocolate chips

Arrange your ingredients on the cake. Leave to set for 30 minutes.

Place a small pink candle on the cake and light it

Imagine your friend meeting the partner of their dreams.

Blow out the candle and make your wish. Remove Candle.

Place cake in a decorative box and give to your friend.

Baking just for You

Does the thought of giving a party leave you cold? Then follow the main recipe as instructed.

Ingredients

Follow instructions from the recipe of your choice.

Before Baking

Make enough mixture for a batch of six cakes and separate an individual portion. Add the ingredients to your mixture following the recipe of your choice.

To Decorate

Follow instructions from the recipe of your choice.

Place a small candle (use coloured candle from the recipe of your choice) **on the cake and light it.**

Blow out the candle and make your wish. Remove Candle.

Follow the instruction in the recipe.

Gift Boxes

If you bake a cake for a friend or lover then presentation is all part of the magic. There is a whole range of cupcake boxes on the market. Continue the magic by selecting a box to match your cake.

To help carry the special thoughts you put into your baking, choose a box in your cake candle colour.

When the gathering comes to an end, there will be much speculation and excitement. Talk about any successes or possible potential candidates will be the topic of conversation over the next few days and weeks. The excitement you create will continue long after the party is over.

The power of a wish can be instantaneous.

The influence of magic might take a little longer.

Believe it will be and dreams can come true.

We are always interested to know about your party successes. Did you or your friends find true love?

Please write a review and tell us about the fun you had.

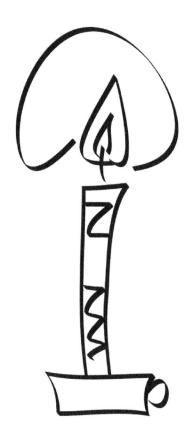